This book belongs to:

....

....

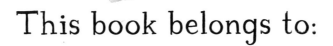

Quarto is the authority on a wide range of topics.
Quarto educates, entertains and enriches the lives of
our readers—enthusiasts and lovers of hands-on living.
www.quartoknows.com

Author: Leonie Roberts
Illustrator: Mike Byrne
Editor: Ellie Brough
Designer: Victoria Kimonidou

Copyright © QED Publishing 2018
First published in the UK in 2018 by QED Publishing

Part of The Quarto Group
The Old Brewery
6 Blundell Street
London N7 9BH

A catalogue record for this book is available from
the British Library.

ISBN 978 1 78493 938 0

Printed in China

MIX
Paper from
responsible sources
FSC® C016973

MY COLOURFUL CHAMELEON

Leonie Roberts

Illustrated by Mike Byrne

I have a pet chameleon.
I love her – she's the best!
But Mummy doesn't like her,
she says that she's a pest!

Mum said, "Your pet is trouble!"

"NO," I said, "she's good!

You will see, she's hiding, Mum. Just the way she should."

The trouble is we lose her.
It drives Mum round the bend!

I must admit it's really hard
to spot my little friend.

Mum said, "That pet is trouble. We lose her every day!"

"But Mum," I said, "I love her. Don't take my pet away!"

We lost her in the kitchen...

We lost her late at night...

Daddy spent the
evening searching
for her with a light.

We lost her in the bathroom...

We lost her on the bed...

Mummy almost sat on her and nearly squashed her head!

We lost her in the living room...

We lost her in the car...

I was meant to hold her,
but the journey was too far!

We lost her in the garden...

We lost her in the hall...

She was lying on the staircase
and had curled up in a ball!

I lost her during Show and Tell,
the teacher got quite mad.

She said that I was trouble,
the worst she'd ever had!

Mum said, "She is not trouble.
The problem is her pet!
It keeps on changing colour,
we will take it to the vet."

I told the vet about my pet,
he said that I was right.

She has to change her colour
to stay safe and out of sight.

Mum asked, "How can we find her?
We lose her every day!"

The vet said we must look for eyes,
hers move in every way.

So my pet **ISN'T** trouble!
She really is quite good.
She has to change her colour,
to hide just like she should.

So now my mummy likes her,
because she is so clever.
And our pet chameleon
can live with us

FOREVER.

NEXT STEPS

Discussion and Comprehension

Ask the children the following questions and discuss their answers:
- What did you like most about this story?
- How did the chameleon stay safe?
- Can you name all of the colours that the chameleon turned into?
- What else would you like to find out about chameleons?

Rhyming Words Play

Explain to the children that the story has lots of words that rhyme. This makes it enjoyable to read out loud. Read the book to the children and see if they can supply the rhyming word at the end of each verse. Together, write down a list of the rhyming word pairs. Then ask the children to write down other words that rhyme with those words. Read out the story again putting in some of the children's new words. How funny can they make it?

Camouflage Chameleon

Give the children a large sheet of coloured paper with the outline of a chameleon drawn on it. Give them lots of shiny paper, tissue paper, felt and wool of the same colour. Ask them to cut and stick small pieces of each material on to the chameleon so that she is camouflaged on the paper.